NFL RIVALRIES

COWBOYS VS. REDSKINS

By Paul Bowker

Kaleidoscope
Minneapolis, MN

Your Front Row Seat to the Games

This edition first published in 2020 by Kaleidoscope Publishing, Inc.

For information regarding permission, write to
Kaleidoscope Publishing, Inc.
6012 Blue Circle Drive
Minnetonka, MN 55343

Library of Congress Control Number
2019939142

ISBN
978-1-64519-080-6 (library bound)
978-1-64494-165-2 (paperback)
978-1-64519-181-0 (ebook)

Printed in the United States of America.

TABLE OF CONTENTS

CHAPTER 1

Biggest Game Yet

Washington Redskins fans packed RFK Stadium. It was New Year's Eve 1972. A trip to the Super Bowl was on the line.

It was early in the fourth quarter. Washington held a seven-point lead. Redskins quarterback Billy Kilmer took the snap. He dropped back to pass. The crowd of 53,000 waited.

Redskins defenders were able to keep Cowboys quarterback Roger Staubach from scoring touchdowns in the 1972 game.

The pass traveled 45 yards. It dropped in Charley Taylor's hands. Touchdown! Washington increased its lead. The Redskins just had to hang on. If they won, they would go to their first Super Bowl.

Getting to the Super Bowl was important. But this game had extra meaning. It was against the Dallas Cowboys.

The Redskins and Cowboys were big **rivals**. They had played each other since 1960. But they had never met in a playoff game. The winner would go to Super Bowl VII.

The Cowboys were already champions. They were trying for their third Super Bowl in a row. No team had ever done that.

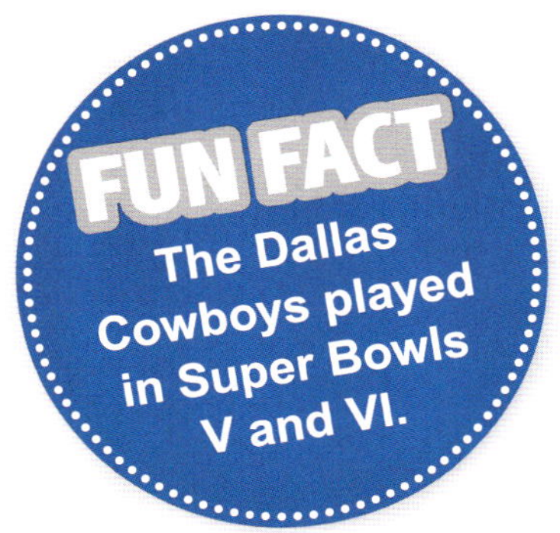

RIGGINS PLOWS AHEAD

John Riggins was a great Redskins running back. One of his best games came against the Cowboys. It was a 1982 playoff game. He carried the ball thirty-six times. He racked up 140 yards. He scored two touchdowns. The Redskins won 31–17. They went on to win their first Super Bowl.

John Riggins wore number 44 for the Redskins.

Redskins players carried coach George Allen off the field after the huge victory.

The Cowboys expected to win. Coach Tom Landry bragged before the game. He said his quarterback was better than Kilmer. But Kilmer had a great game. He completed 14 of 18 passes. He threw two touchdowns.

Redskins kicker Curt Knight made four field goals. He drilled a 45-yarder to finish off the game. Washington won 26–3. The crowd cheered. They poured onto the field to celebrate.

The game added to the rivalry. But there were many more exciting moments to come.

CHAPTER 2

Rivals Since 1960

They called Eddie LeBaron the Little General. He was short for a football player. He stood 5-foot-7 (1.70 m). But he was also a war hero. He fought in the Korean War (1950–1953). He received awards for bravery.

LeBaron played pro football when he returned. He was a quarterback. And he played on both sides of the rivalry. He played for the Redskins in the 1950s. But he was a Cowboy on October 9, 1960. That was the first meeting of the teams. It was the Cowboys' first season.

FUN FACT

LeBaron served as a US Marine during the Korean War.

LeBaron may have been short, but he was a tough player.

The Cowboys traded for LeBaron. They gave up two **draft** picks. LeBaron started out quickly against his old team. He fired a deep pass in the second quarter. It sailed 32 yards. Frank Clarke caught it. The touchdown put Dallas ahead. It was 7–3.

But it was all Redskins from there. Washington won 26–14. But neither team had a good season. It was the only win for the Redskins that year. The Cowboys didn't win any.

The teams went on to become major rivals. They played for league championships. They played on Monday Night Football. They played on Thanksgiving.

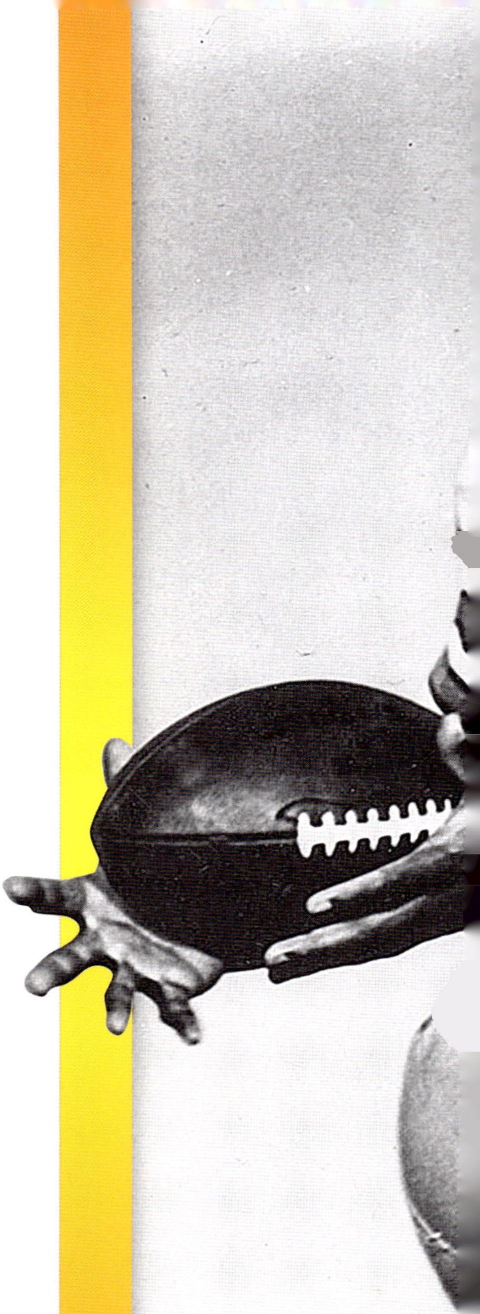

FUN FACT
The Cowboys beat the Redskins for the first time in 1962.

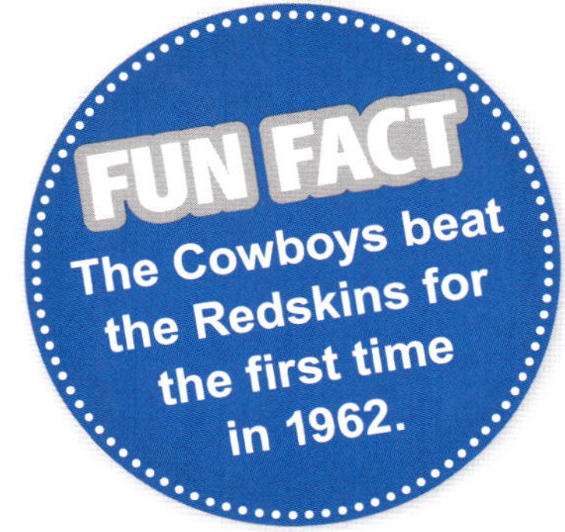

Frank Clarke played in many big games for the Cowboys.

The rivalry began because of a song. Clint Murchison was a Texas businessman. He wanted to start a pro football team. He needed the approval of all the team owners. The Redskins owner was George Preston Marshall. He opposed a new team.

But Murchison had something Marshall wanted. He owned the rights to the Redskins fight song. The song was called "Hail to the Redskins." Murchison would give up the rights. But only if Preston voted yes. He did. Preston got his song. And Murchison got his football team. The Cowboys were born.

Marshall had owned the Redskins since 1932.

Rivalry Map

Washington Redskins
FedExField
Landover, Maryland
Montana
North Dakota
Minnesota
Wisconsin
South Dakota
Wyoming
Michigan
New York
Iowa
Nebraska
Pennsylvania
Illinois
Indiana
Ohio
Colorado
West Virginia
Kansas
Missouri
Virginia
Kentucky
North Carolina
Tennessee
New Mexico
Oklahoma
Arkansas
South Carolina
Mississippi
Alabama
Georgia
Dallas Cowboys
AT&T Stadium
Arlington, Texas
Louisiana
Florida
N
W
E
S

CHAPTER 3

Turkey Day Triumph

Clint Longley stood on the **sidelines**. It was Thanksgiving Day 1974. Longley was a **backup** quarterback for the Cowboys. He would only play if something happened to the starter.

Roger Staubach was the starter. The Cowboys were trailing the Redskins. It was 16–3. The Thanksgiving game was a big one. It was a Dallas tradition. The Cowboys play a Thanksgiving game every year.

It was the third quarter. Staubach got the ball. He was hit hard by Dave Robinson. He had to leave the game. In came Longley.

The Redskins went after Cowboys quarterback Roger Staubach. He was knocked out of the game.

Longley showed off two newspapers that talked about his amazing play in the Thanksgiving game.

"I was a little bit scared," Longley said.

It didn't look like it. Longley threw the ball up. Billy Joe Dupree caught it for a touchdown. That score made it 16–10.

Now it was late in the game. The Cowboys still trailed. It was 23–17. Some fans began to leave. They thought the game was over. Only 28 seconds remained. Longley stepped back to pass. He picked out Drew Pearson. He launched the ball downfield. Pearson caught it. Touchdown!

The Cowboys kicked the **extra point**. They won 24–23. Longley became a rivalry hero in just one game. There have been many other rivalry stars.

Don Meredith was a Cowboys quarterback. He played from 1960 to 1968. He played the Redskins fifteen times. In 1967, the Cowboys were behind 14–10. Only 18 seconds were left. It was fourth down. Meredith hit Dan Reeves with a pass. Reeves ran into the **end zone**. The Cowboys won.

John Riggins was a Redskins running back. He had 1,157 career rushing yards against the Cowboys. That was more than against any other team. The division title was on the line in 1984. Riggins got the ball. He plowed into the end zone from 1 yard out. The touchdown came in the fourth quarter. It gave the Redskins a 30–28 win.

FUN FACT

The Redskins won their first eleven games in 1991. The first team to beat them was the Cowboys.

HEAD TO HEAD

STATS

Through the 2018 season

WASHINGTON		DALLAS
43	WINS	71
37.9	WINNING PERCENTAGE	62.1
2,238	POINTS SCORED	2,709
2	PLAYOFF WINS	0
4 (1986–88)	LONGEST WIN STREAK	(1997–02) 10
3	TOTAL SUPER BOWL VICTORIES	5

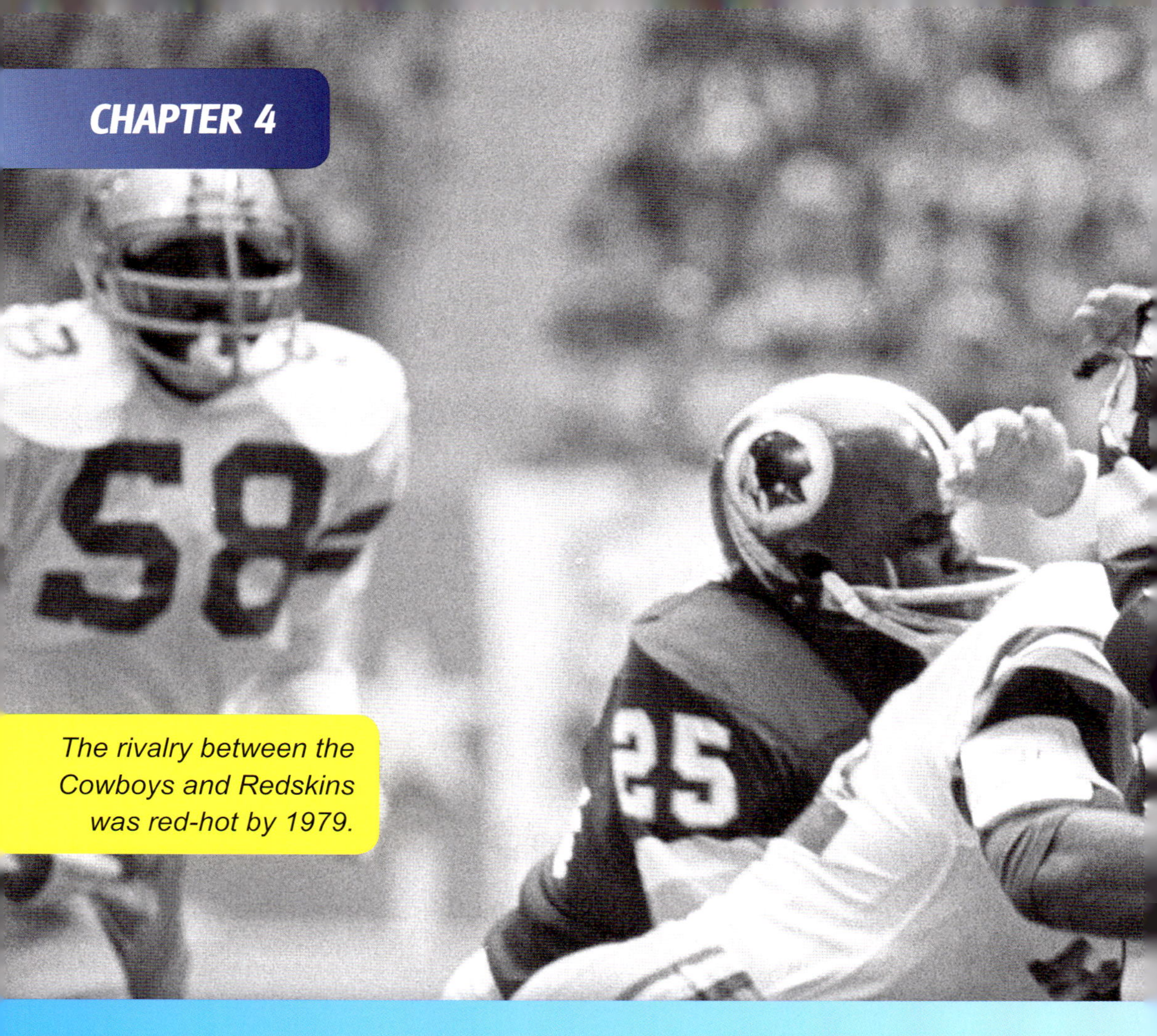

The rivalry between the Cowboys and Redskins was red-hot by 1979.

Insults

It was 1979. A special delivery showed up for the Cowboys. It came from an address in Maryland. It was a funeral wreath. A Redskins fan had sent it as a joke. He sent it for the Cowboys' loss to the Redskins. But it was still days before the game.

Cowboys defensive end Harvey Martin was angry. He took the wreath. He put it in front of his locker. It made him want to beat the Redskins even more. The upcoming game was a big one. There was a three-way tie for first place. The Cowboys and Redskins were two of the teams.

Game day came. The Cowboys fell behind 17–0. Then Dallas woke up. The Cowboys tied the game at 17. Then Washington rallied. The Cowboys trailed 34–28. There was 2:20 left in the game.

Roger Staubach led a **drive**. He led the Cowboys 75 yards. He threw a touchdown pass to Tony Hill. The Cowboys won 35–34. So much for the wreath.

The teams battled back and forth in the December 1979 game.

THE WINNING TOUCHDOWN

Tony Hill lined up at the right side of the line on the winning touchdown play. He ran ahead into the end zone. Staubach received the snap. Then he threw just a moment later. The ball sailed through the air. Hill caught it in the back corner of the end zone. He raised his hands over his head in celebration as he ran out of the end zone.

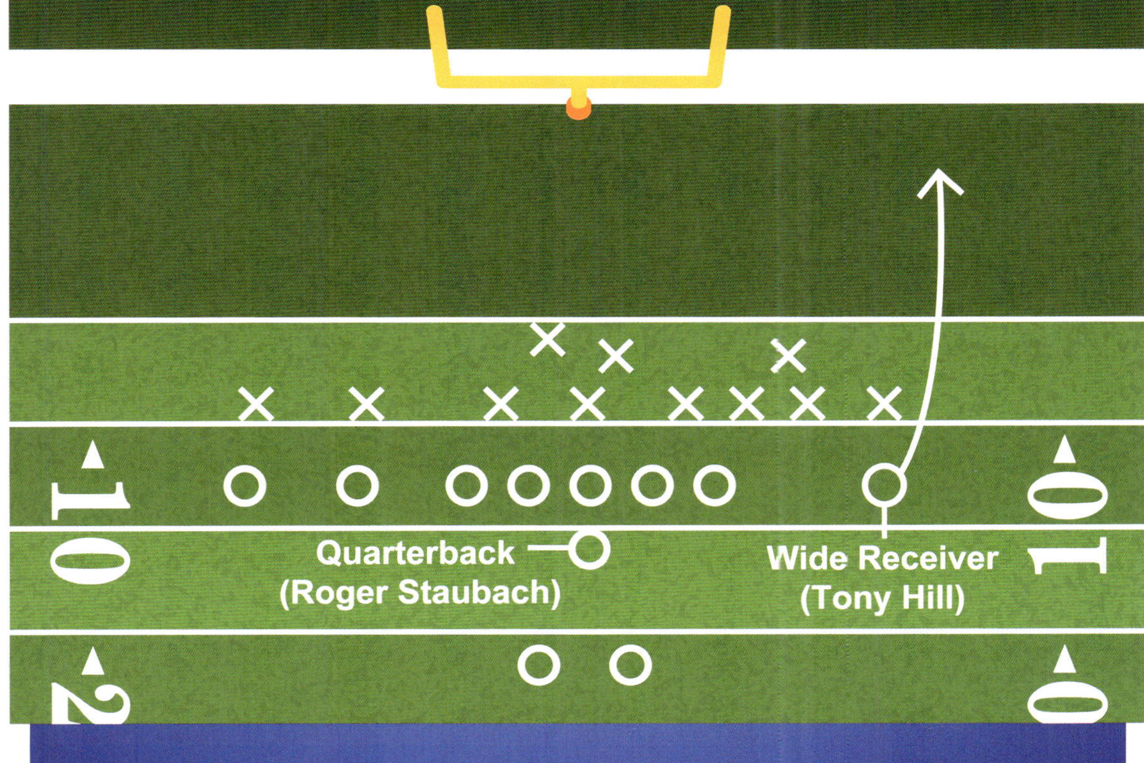

Martin carries the wreath back to the Redskins locker room after the big win.

The Cowboys celebrated their win. Martin went into the locker room. He grabbed the wreath. Then he walked over to the Redskins locker room. He tossed the wreath inside.

The Cowboys and Redskins have played in many big games. But even ordinary games are special. It is part of the history of the rivalry.

FUN FACT

Tom Landry coached the Cowboys for 29 years. The last win of his career was against the Redskins in 1988.

FAREWELL GAME

Washington's home for 36 seasons was RFK Stadium. The final game at RFK was against the Cowboys. It was on December 22, 1996. The Redskins won 37–10. Washington won more than 60 percent of its games at RFK.

BEYOND THE BOOK

After reading the book, it's time to think about what you learned. Try the following exercises to jumpstart your ideas.

THINK

THAT'S NEWS TO ME. Chapter One talks about the first playoff game between the Cowboys and Redskins in 1972. How might news sources be able to fill in more detail about this? What new information could you find in news articles? Where could you go to find those sources?

CREATE

SHARPEN YOUR RESEARCH SKILLS. Chapter Two mentions the song "Hail to the Redskins." Dallas team owner Clint Murchison gave up his rights to the song so that he could get a vote from the Redskins in favor of his new team. Where could you go in the library to find more information about this? Who could you talk to who might know more? Create a research plan. Write a paragraph about your next steps.

SHARE

WHAT'S YOUR OPINION? The book states that the Cowboys and Redskins formed one of the best rivalries in pro football. Do you agree or disagree with this position? Use evidence from the text to support your answer. Share your position and evidence with a friend. Does your friend agree with you?

GROW

REAL-LIFE RESEARCH. What places would you go to learn more about the rivalry between the Cowboys and the Redskins? What other things could you learn while you were there?

RESEARCH NINJA

Visit www.ninjaresearcher.com/0806 to learn how to take your research skills and book report writing to the next level!

RESEARCH

SEARCH LIKE A PRO

Learn about how to use search engines to find useful websites.

FACT OR FAKE?

Discover how you can tell a trusted website from an untrustworthy resource.

TEXT DETECTIVE

Explore how to zero in on the information you need most.

SHOW YOUR WORK

Research responsibly—learn how to cite sources.

WRITE

GET TO THE POINT

Learn how to express your main ideas.

PLAN OF ATTACK

Learn prewriting exercises and create an outline.

DOWNLOADABLE REPORT FORMS

Further Resources

BOOKS

Mack, Larry. *The Dallas Cowboys Story*. Bellwether Media, 2017.

Mack, Larry. *The Washington Redskins Story*. Bellwether Media, 2017.

Wilner, Barry. *NFL's Top Ten Rivalries*. Abdo Publishing, 2018.

WEBSITES

Factsurfer.com gives you a safe, fun way to find more information.

1. Go to www.factsurfer.com.
2. Enter "Cowboys vs. Redskins" into the search box and click 🔍.
3. Select your book cover to see a list of related websites.

Glossary

backup: A backup player is one who only plays if another player cannot. Clint Longley was the backup quarterback for the Cowboys.

draft: A draft is how teams choose new players to add to their rosters. The Cowboys traded two draft picks for Eddie LeBaron.

drive: The series of plays an offense runs while it has the ball is called a drive. Roger Staubach led the Cowboys on a long scoring drive.

end zone: The end zone is where players must reach to score a touchdown. Each football field has two end zones.

extra point: The extra point is a kick attempt that takes place after a team scores a touchdown. The Redskins made the extra point to tie the game.

rivals: Rivals are two teams or athletes that play a lot and badly want to beat the other. The Cowboys and Redskins have been rivals since 1960.

sidelines: The areas located along both sides of the football field are the sidelines. Players who are not in the game stand on the sidelines.

Index

PHOTO CREDITS

The images in this book are reproduced through the courtesy of: Al Tielemans/AP Images, front cover (left); Eric Christian Smith/AP Images, front cover (right); EFKS/Shutterstock Images, front cover (background); Jeff Bukowski/Shutterstock Images, pp. 3 (left), 3 (right), 27; Arnie Sachs/picture–alliance/dpa/AP Images, pp. 4–5; Tony Tomsic/AP Images, p. 7; AP Images, pp. 8, 11, 14, 22–23, 24; David Lee/Shutterstock Images, p. 9; Corporal Peter McDonald/US Marine Corps/Wikimedia Commons, p. 10; NFL Photos/AP Images, pp. 12–13, 16–17; Red Line Editorial, pp. 15, 21; Harold Waters/AP Images, pp. 18–19; Danny E Hooks/Shutterstock Images, p. 20; enterlinedesign/Shutterstock Images, p. 25; Jerry Hoefer/AP Images, p. 26; Mtsaride/Shutterstock Images, p. 30.

ABOUT THE AUTHOR

Paul Bowker is a sports editor and children's book author who was raised in Massachusetts and is now living in Mississippi. He has covered hundreds of NFL games, including many games involving the Redskins and Cowboys.